The Case of the Disappearing Dirt

Dandi Daley Mackall
Illustrated by Kay Salem

This book is dedicated
to J. W. Daley, "Uncle Jack."
Thanks for being a fan for all these years!

The Scripture quotation is taken from the HOLY BIBLE, NEW INTERNATIONAL VERSION®. NIV®. Copyright © 1973, 1978, 1984 by International Bible Society. Used by permission of Zondervan Publishing House. All rights reserved.

Copyright © 1996 Dandi Daley Mackall
Published by Concordia Publishing House
3558 S. Jefferson Avenue, St. Louis, MO 63118-3968
Manufactured in the United States of America

Library of Congress Cataloging-in-Publication Data

Mackall, Dandi Daley.
    The case of the disappearing Dirt / Dandi Daley Mackall.
        p.   cm. — (Cinnamon Lake mysteries)
        Summary: When the tagalong member of their club disappears, Molly and the other members begin a search which gets scary and causes them to question their responsibility in the matter.
        ISBN 0-570-04793-5
        [1. Missing persons—Fiction. 2. Responsibility—Fiction. 3. Christian life—Fiction. 4. Mystery and detective stories.]
    I. Title. II. Series.
PZ7.M1905Cas   1996
[Fic]—dc20   96-14003

2 3 4 5 6 7 8 9 10   05 04 03 02 01 00 99 98 97

Cinnamon Lake Mysteries

*I'm not sure how we got famous
as the Cinnamon Lake Mystery Club.
I mean, the Cinnamon Lake part
is easy. That's where we live.
The mystery part is more ...
mysterious.*

Contents

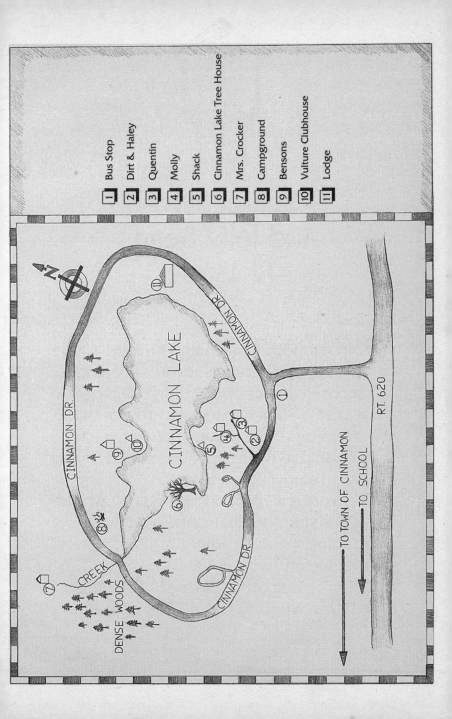

1 Bus Stop
2 Dirt & Haley
3 Quentin
4 Molly
5 Shack
6 Cinnamon Lake Tree House
7 Mrs. Crocker
8 Campground
9 Bensons
10 Vulture Clubhouse
11 Lodge

CINNAMON LAKE

CINNAMON DR.

CINNAMON DR.

CINNAMON DR.

CREEK

DENSE WOODS

RT. 620

TO TOWN OF CINNAMON

TO SCHOOL

N

Scarecrows
and Jelly Beans
12:45 P.M.

"Dirt, stop it!" I pleaded with her. "I have to learn my lines. Tryouts are in three hours."

I scooted as far from Dirt as you can get in a bus seat. School had let out early for teachers meetings. We were halfway back to Cinnamon Lake already. I needed every minute to study.

Dirt leaned across and pushed up our window. Dirt's not her real name. But since she wants to be someone who digs up bones and stuff for history, we call her Dirt.

"Dirt," I begged. "Please?" She knew I hated the window open. But she didn't shut it.

Mr. Winkle, our bus driver, hit the same pothole he hits every day. My playbook fell to the floor. The few lines I thought I had bumped out of my head.

Dirt raised her voice. "Cinnamon Elementary presents *The Wizard of Oz,* starring Molly Mack." Dirt paused and yawned. "Nope," she said. "Can't see it."

I tried to ignore her. *And* what she said. But I was having trouble seeing myself win the part too. It was only September. Already I hadn't made the soccer team. I didn't get third grade cheerleader or student council. And I didn't get past the first round of the spelling bee. Just another average year for Molly Mack.

But I wanted to win the part of Dorothy more than all the other stuff put together. I might have a chance this time. I look a *little* like Dorothy.

I practiced the tryout lines. *A tornado sweeps Dorothy to Oz. She hugs her dog.* "Oh, Toto. We're not in Kansas anymore. Oh, Toto. We're—"

"Hey, Molly," Dirt broke in. "Look what Mrs. Francis wrote on my homework. She doesn't like my *S*'s. Show me how to do it her way."

Mrs. Francis is Dirt's first grade teacher. Dirt scribbled a few snakes on her tablet.

I closed my eyes and whispered to myself. "Oh, Toto. We're not in Kansas—"

"Molly, do it!" Dirt tugged on my shirt.

When I looked down, I saw her full, gross, sticky handprint on my sleeve. It looked like oil and chocolate, mixed.

"Dirt!" I cried. "Now look what you did! This is my only Kansas sunflower shirt!"

Dirt shoved her short, chopped hair out of her eyes. "I don't see why you want to be in that dumb play. All Dorothy does is skip to Oz. I'd rather be Scarecrow. Besides, Haley's got that Dorothy part sewn up."

Haley is the prettiest girl in our class. She's also Dirt's big sister. Usually, they act like they don't know each other. Haley was Cinderella in second grade and Snow Queen in first. I was a mouse and a snowflake.

"Well," I said, trying to believe my own words, "Mr. Adams has not given out parts yet. So I have just as good a chance as Haley."

Dirt smirked. "Yeah, right."

That did it.

"Get out!" I said. "Move!"

Dirt didn't budge. "Move yourself, Scarecrow." My shirt was dirty. My hair was blowing all over. Thanks to Dirt and the open window, I *felt* like a scarecrow. I jumped to my feet and picked up my backpack.

"Hey!" Dirt said. "What about my *S*'s?"

"Do your own *S*'s!" I said. "You're not my responsibility. You … you …" I couldn't think of anything to call her. "Dirt!"

I looked around for Quentin. He had claimed the seat behind Mr. Winkle. His nose was buried in his science book.

There were two empty seats—one beside Ben Benson. (I'd squirt ketchup in my eyes before I'd sit by him.) The other was by Haley. I chose Haley.

"Oooh," she whined, when I plopped next to her. "Don't touch me. You're dirty!"

Haley eyed my playbook. "Molly," she said,"are *you* trying out?"

I wished I'd sat by Ben. "Yeah," I mumbled.

Sam Benson, Ben's younger brother, popped up behind us. "What part are you going for, Molly? Toto? The dog?" He and Haley burst out laughing.

Sam was the Prince in Cinderella. I think he would have made a better wicked step-brother.

I wheeled around to face Sam. That's when I saw Marty's giant hand reach in. Marty is the leader of the Vultures, a club that does nothing but give us Cinnamon Lakers trouble. Up went Haley's pink, ballerina lunchbox.

"No fair!" Haley screamed.

Marty tossed the lunchbox over his head to his partner in crime, Ben Benson. Ben caught it and threw it to Eric the Red. Eric held it over his shaggy, red hair.

Haley made a grab for her lunch. She missed and fell on the little kid in front of us.

"Get off!" he squeaked.

"I want my lunchbox," Haley whined. "Give it back! I'll tell—"

Just then, Marty caught it. He swung it around by the handle. The lunchbox flew open. Out poured empty Baggies, half-eaten sandwiches, grape juice, and a whole bag of jelly beans.

Kids jumped out of their seats. Jelly beans flew everywhere. All the kids yelled. Mr. Winkle yelled something too. He glared into

10

his rearview mirror. One bus wheel strayed off the road. He jerked the bus back in the lane.

Kids tumbled into other kids. Haley was knocked off her feet. She started crying.

Mr. Winkle slammed on the brakes. He stood up and said, "Be quiet! I can't see where I'm going." Everyone quieted down. We knew we'd better stay that way.

Just inside Cinnamon Lake, Mr. Winkle came to a screeching stop. He cranked open the bus door. Kids tramped out the door. Everybody slipped on jelly beans.

"Bye, Mr. Winkle," I said as I hopped down the bus steps.

I'm not sure what a bus driver is supposed to look like. But I'm sure it's not like Mr. Winkle. He reminds me of a nervous Humpty Dumpty. I'm afraid he's going to roll right off the driver's seat and break into a million pieces. Mr. Winkle was mumbling, *"Friday. Three days to Friday."*

"Molly!" Quentin came up behind me. Sometimes he walks home with me to see if my mom will give him junk food. There's no junk food at Quentin's house.

"What time is the Cinnamon Laker meeting?"

he asked.

I'd forgotten. "Not today, Quentin. Tryouts are at four o'clock. Aren't you trying out for the play this afternoon?"

"Hardly," he said. "Did you ever hear of an African American Oz? I wouldn't fit in Tin Man's costume. And who would believe me as a scarecrow with no brains?"

Quentin's going to be a scientist when he grows up. He has a very big brain. Most of Quentin is pretty big. Especially his belly.

"Let's change the meeting to tomorrow," I said. "Haley's trying out too."

Quentin and I walked together. He read. I tried to learn my lines, but I couldn't. Talking about Haley made me think of Dirt.

"You know," I said, "Dirt Harrison never asks for help. She must really be having trouble with *S*'s. Maybe I ought to call her."

"Hmmm." Quentin was studying the sky now. A few gray puffs were moving fast.

"I must get home to check the weather vane," he said. "This may be our coldest September on record."

I felt a chill as I walked home alone, past tall evergreens whose tips swayed in the breeze. It took me longer than usual because

I worked on Dorothy's speech.

The second I stepped into the house, the phone rang. "Hello?" I said.

"Molly?"

"Haley! I was just about to call Dirt."

"That's just it!" Haley said. Her voice sounded shaky. "Dirt is missing!"

The Search Begins
1:16 P.M.

"What do you mean Dirt's missing?" I sent Haley's words back to her through the phone.

"Gone. Oooh, Mother will kill me if I've lost Dirt."

"Haley, are you sure Dirt didn't just beat you home? Maybe she's come and gone already."

Dirt and Haley aren't far from the bus stop. It takes Dirt two minutes to get home, change, and dash outside.

"She never got home!" Haley said. "Kelsey is baby-sitting until Mom gets off work. She says I'm the first one here."

"Dirt can take care of herself," I said.

"She's probably hunting tadpoles."

I checked the kitchen clock. "Haley, I need to study my lines."

"But—"

"Listen," I said, feeling a little sorry that I'd snapped at Dirt on the bus, "if Dirt doesn't turn up in 15 minutes, call me back." That seemed to satisfy her. She hung up. I got back to my playbook.

But first I needed a snack. My Snickers. I'd saved it from Saturday. Just what I needed to give my little gray cells energy. Quentin calls *thinking* using your little gray cells.

I raced to the kitchen, my stomach aching for the candy bar.

"Mom!" I called. "I'm home!"

Instead of Mom, Tiffany stood in the kitchen. I'd forgotten about Tiffany, the teenaged baby-sitter. I don't know why Mom and Dad think I still need a baby-sitter. I'm no baby. And Tiffany wouldn't know if I'm sitting or skydiving.

Tiffany had her head stuck into the refrigerator. One hand grasped the open door. In that hand, I saw my half-eaten Snickers.

"Oh, hi," she said when she saw me. "Molly, do you have any root beer?"

"I don't think so," I said. "Where's Chuckie?"

"Huh?" Tiffany stuck her head back in the frig.

"My little brother?" I said louder.

"Um, I think he must be at the day-care center," she said. "Um, that's what Mrs. Mack said. Oh yeah. And she said to tell you she'd get home in time to take you to tryouts."

Tiffany settled for a can of 7UP. "Well, bye," she said.

She headed for the den—and the phone. I knew I wouldn't see her again until Mom came home.

Ah well. Now I could practice those lines. Land of Oz, here I come.

I started on the second set of lines Mr. Adams gave us for Dorothy. It was where she gets mad at the cowardly lion for scaring Toto. I said the words over and over to myself. Then aloud.

Once I looked at the clock. It had been longer than 15 minutes since I talked with Haley. Dirt must have come home.

I went back to the playbook. I was still going strong when I heard a loud knock on the door. *Bamm! Bamm! Bamm!*

Wild elephants could knock the door down, and Tiffany would never answer it. I got up. As soon as I touched the doorknob, the door flung open. In stormed Haley.

"Molly!" she whined, pushing me aside. "I've been trying to call you! Is your phone broken?"

"No," I said. "It must still be on Tiffany's ear."

"Dirt's still not home. I was supposed to walk home with her from the bus stop. Mother will be so mad at me if we can't find my sister! She'll say it's my fault."

"Did you check the woods, Haley? Dirt's shortcut?"

"No," Haley admitted. "I hate going that way. There are stickers! You go, Molly."

I took a deep breath and set down my playbook, still opened to Dorothy's part. "Okay," I said, "I'll find her. But you're going with me."

We cut across the field to get to Dirt's path. It was cool enough to make me wish I'd brought my jacket. The leaves weren't turning red and yellow yet. But some leaves had fallen to the ground. They crunched when we walked.

"It's not like Dirt," Haley said. She was panting, but she kept up with me. "Dirt always comes home and eats prunes and peanut butter. Then she goes out again."

"Prunes and peanut butter?"

"In an ice cream cone," Haley added.

I shook my head. What could happen to a kid who ate peanut butter-and-prune cones?

We came to a big ditch. I grabbed a huge Tarzan vine. Dirt had showed us how to do it. Then I took a running start and jumped.

"Dirt!" I yelled as I sailed over the ditch. Nobody answered.

Haley called out "Dirt" from her side of the ditch. I hollered from mine. Nothing. A woodpecker made a *rat-tat-tat* noise. Behind me a squirrel stirred up leaves, then raced up a pine tree.

"Haley!" I yelled across the ditch. "You better go back and ask if anybody's seen Dirt. I'll keep looking here."

Haley turned to go.

"And bring Quentin back with you!" I yelled.

I started off into the woods, toward the campground. Every few steps I called out, "Dirt!"

"Hey! You there!"

The man's voice made my heart stop. I looked around but couldn't see anybody. I felt like a trapped deer, with a hunter aiming at me from behind a bush.

"You! What do you want?" he said.

Then I saw him. It was Bingo Bob, the groundskeeper. Everybody calls him Bingo Bob because he calls out the numbers when the camp has Bingo nights. He was dumping mowed grass in the forest.

"You looking for Dirt?" he asked.

"Yes, I am. Have you seen her?"

He lifted his baseball cap and scratched his head. "Can't say I have. She might be feeding her bats. Or maybe working on the anthill."

"She might be *where?* Doing *what?*" I asked. I didn't know Dirt had bats or ants.

"She comes by here every night. She feeds three baby bats with an eyedropper. Don't ask me what she feeds them. The anthill is one I wrecked mowing. Dirt's fixing it back up."

Bingo Bob told me where to look, but Dirt wasn't there. I found the anthill. But I didn't find the bats. Thank goodness.

I decided to try the creek. I should have

gone there right away! Dirt would be there catching tadpoles or crawdads. Then I could get back to business.

As I tore through the woods to the creek, I half expected Dirt to jump out from behind a tree. When she didn't, I started to pray she would.

Tracking Dirt
1:35 P.M.

I had just made it to the creek when I heard my name called.

"Molly! Molly Mack!"

"I'm here, Haley! The creek!"

When the lake gets full, it flows into ditches that make little creeks. This was Dirt's favorite. The muddiest. I'd never admit it, but this part of the woods scared me a little. If Cinnamon Lake had bears or lions, this is where they would live.

"Molly?" Quentin yelled. His voice cracked on the last part.

"Quick!" I hollered back. "This way!"

I could hear Quentin and Haley plodding through the forest. I picked up a stick and poked around in the mud. It hadn't rained for a couple of days. But it was still muddy by the creek bed. I could make out a few animal tracks.

"I asked everybody," Haley said. "Even Ben Benson! Nobody's seen Dirt." She was trying to pick little, green stickers out of her long, blonde hair.

Quentin grabbed onto tree limbs to get down to the creek bank. He still had on his school pants. But he'd added a raincoat.

"Molly Mack," he said, "I was in the middle of an important experiment. You have led me into the woods to find Dirt? Have you lost what remains of your senses?"

"You think I want to be here?" I said. "I still have half the lines to read over before I can try out for Dorothy!"

"Then let's go home," Quentin said.

"I know it sounds dumb," I admitted. "But Dirt's disappeared. *Nobody's* seen her."

"Perhaps she does not wish to be seen," he said. Quentin ran his stubby fingers through his short, black hair.

"Just help us find her, Quentin. Then I can get back to my playbook. And you can get back to your experiment."

"And I can get back to—" Haley paused, as if she couldn't think what she had to get back to. "Well," she explained, "I've already learned the tryout lines. I'm starting to work on all of Dorothy's part for the play."

I really had to find Dirt and get back to studying. "Haley," I asked, remembering what Bingo Bob told me, "did you know Dirt comes here at night and feeds bats?"

"No," she said, "but it doesn't surprise me. Mother gave up trying to get Dirt to bed on time. Who knows what she does after we fall asleep."

I bent down by the animal tracks. "Quentin, come here and look at these."

With my stick I pointed out a large print that looked like two giant teardrops, side by side. "These are deer tracks. Right?"

"Correct," Quentin said. He sighed and looked at his watch.

A little farther down the creek, we ran into a bunch of animal tracks.

"Look at these!" I shouted. "Weird. Something must have scared the animals." Tracks that were close together got farther apart. "It looks like they took off running!"

"I think this one is a rabbit track," I said.

There were two large footprints and two small ones, each with four toes. Since I figured the big ones were the back feet, I started following the tracks west, the way it looked like the rabbit had fled.

"Miss Detective?" Quentin called.

I didn't look up but kept following the tracks. If something scared the rabbit, maybe it had also scared Dirt. Maybe she ran in the same direction.

"Oh, Miss Detective?" Quentin said again.

"What is it, Quentin?"

"You are going backwards," he said.

"No, I'm not," I said. I figured maybe Quentin's gray cells weren't working today.

"The front feet would indeed be the lead feet if a rabbit chose to walk. In case you have failed to notice, rabbits do not walk. They hop. In so doing, they thrust their large back feet in front of their small front paws."

It made sense. Quentin was right as usual. I was tracking backwards. I turned around and tried to track the rabbit. After awhile, the prints disappeared into the bushes. So we went back to the creek.

Haley picked up something from the ground. "What do you suppose this is?" she asked. In her hand lay several white, broken, hard things.

Quentin took a look. "I would say you are holding the remains of a raccoon dinner. Crayfish bones."

"Yuk!" Haley screamed and dropped the bones. "Oh, ick! This is all Dirt's fault. I'm going to make her pay for this."

We kept walking until we landed on a real find. Tracks ran all over the place. Quentin and I went to work figuring them out.

"Two raccoons!" I hollered. I can usually pick out raccoon tracks because they look like handprints and footprints of a baby with long fingernails.

"I found tracks of two squirrels and one chipmunk," Quentin announced. "They're all going in the same direction. Toward your raccoons."

My stomach began churning, like it does when I have to answer a question in class. We tracked the animal prints for several yards. *Dear God,* I prayed, *please help us find Dirt.*

Then I spotted the strangest tracks yet. There in the mud, plain as day, was the shape of a foot with a big toe and four little toes. "It's Dirt!" I screamed.

Haley and Quentin came running. "Where is she?" Haley yelled. "She is in so much trouble!"

"Not Dirt," I explained. "Her footprint!"

Quentin examined the mud. "Bare feet. Human. Small. I believe it is safe to conclude this belongs to the person in question."

"Now all we have to do is follow her footprints," I said. I felt good again. It was silly to worry about Dirt. How could we have thought she'd gotten herself lost? Dirt, for crying out loud!

"So let's find her," I said. "I've still got time to get back and go over lines. But we better step on it."

Quentin led the way, explaining what he saw in the footprints. It was as if he were reading a book to us. "Dirt comes to the creek," he said. "She is joined by two raccoons. One on her left. One on her right."

Each step in the mud made a squishy sound. I followed Quentin. Haley kept up with us from the top of the bank, well out of the mud. I could see a story in the tracks. Dirt walked in the middle of the animals. They moved at the same speed. Then all at once the two sets of raccoon prints stopped. They just disappeared.

"Quentin, what happened?" I asked.

Haley called down from the bank of the creek, "What?"

"Very strange," Quentin muttered.

"What's very strange?" Haley cried.

"There's only one explanation," Quentin said. "Raccoons do not take off and fly. Dirt must have picked them up."

"Dirt picked up two coons?" I asked.

"And carried them with her."

We tracked without talking for awhile. My own words popped into my head. *You're not my responsibility. You ... Dirt.* I wished I could have those words back.

I remembered a cartoon I saw once. The characters kept their heads down following somebody's footprints. They ran smack into the person they were looking for. I hoped we would do the same thing.

It didn't happen. Instead, I heard Quentin moan. "Oh no!" he said.

I ran up to him. "Quentin, what is it?"

Quentin pointed. The tracks led to the scariest place in all Cinnamon Lake. Maybe the scariest place in the whole county. The whole world.

"The cave!" I whispered.

We called it the cave. It was really more like a tunnel. The huge stone pipe ran underground. Dirt told me once that some rich guy planned to build a palace. But he changed his mind. All he left was the tunnel. We used to dare each other to climb through to the other side. None of us ever made it. Except Dirt.

I had tried two or three times. Each time I'd turned back because of slime or cobwebs. It was so gross and scary, I never got farther than a few feet.

"This is where I draw the line," Quentin said.

"Don't look at me!" Haley said, picking her way down the creek bank to us. "I'd rather have Mother kill me than to go in there."

I tried to see inside the cave. The pipe ran straight, then curved. Nothing but black deep inside. "Dirt!" I yelled into the pipe.

The cry echoed: *Dirt ... Dirt ... Dirt.*

No answer. I couldn't just leave her in there. Maybe something awful had happened to her. Maybe the animals turned on her and she couldn't get out. Maybe ...

I whispered a quick prayer. "Okay," I said, "I'm going in."

Fright at the End
of the Tunnel
1:55 P.M.

"Did I hear you correctly?" Quentin asked me. "Are you actually planning to enter the tunnel?" Quentin had watched me chicken out of that tunnel more than once.

"We can't just leave Dirt there," I said.

"Dirt loves the cave," Haley said. She peeked over my shoulder into the tunnel.

"I know," I said. "But why isn't she answering? I *have* to go in."

"It is a shame we do not have a rope," Quentin said. "We could tie it around your ankle. They used to do it to priests who entered the inner temple of Jerusalem once a year. If the priest fainted, nobody could go in and get him. So they tied a rope around his ankle. That way they could pull him out."

That did a lot for my courage. Maybe I should try out for the cowardly lion.

"Go the long way around," I said. "Meet me at the other end."

I had to duck my head to step into the tunnel. If I stuck my arms out all the way, I could touch the sides. "Gross!" I hollered. My left hand touched something slimy. I wiped it on my jeans.

"Are you all right, Molly?" Quentin yelled in.

The sound was so loud inside the tunnel, my ears hurt. "Just be on the other side!" I said. My own words bounced back at me.

I heard their footsteps shuffle, then fade. I made myself put one foot in front of the other. It smelled like my closet when I leave my wet bathing suit in it.

My head passed through something soft and sticky. It clung to my hair and my nose. I wiped madly at it. Spider webs! I'd walked into the Empire State Building of spiders! I only hoped the spiders were out.

"Dirt?" I called. But I knew I'd get no answer. *Where are you, Dirt?*

My next step landed with a *squish!* I almost slid down. Trying not to imagine what I'd stepped on, I made myself keep going. Ahead of me was a scratching sound.

"Shoo!" I yelled. The scritch-scratching grew louder, then faded. Something—mice? rats? muskrats?—darted out ahead of me. I wanted to turn back. I wanted out of there. But I closed my eyes and kept walking.

I opened my eyes. The cave looked the same either way. Black. I couldn't see a thing. After a few minutes that felt like hours, I saw a light. Light at the end of the tunnel. I was going to make it!

I felt mud and slime tugging at my gym shoes. Then I was sloshing in water up to my ankles. I tried not to think about snakes as I took my last steps in the cave.

Finally I stepped onto grass. I stood up straight. Never had it felt so good to be outside! Even though the whole sky was covered with clouds, I had to squint. It felt bright to me.

My white shoes had turned brown, with specks of slime green. I smelled like the cave.

Only then did I look around to see where I was. I gasped. I was standing in the backyard of old Mrs. Crocker. *Off-Her-Rocker Crocker!*

Mom told me never to call her that. But the stories I'd heard made me think it was a good name for her. Nobody ever came near her house.

I peered across the lawn and into the open window. A shadow moved inside the house. I ran to the nearest tree and crouched behind it.

Something touched my shoulder. I jumped and banged my head into the tree trunk.

"Molly?" Quentin whispered.

Quentin and Haley stared down at me.

"You stink," Haley said.

"Any sign of Dirt?" Quentin asked.

"No," I said. "But look where we are."

Quentin glanced at the house. "It's not—"

"It is," I said.

"Where?" Haley shouted.

"*Shhh!* It's Mrs. Crocker's house, Haley," I said.

Haley's face turned whiter than usual. "Off-Her-Rocker Crocker?"

We hid, huddled close together behind the oak tree. I shivered. It might have been the wind. It might have been my wet shoes.

It might have been fear.

"We have to move in closer," I whispered. I picked a cottonwood tree just a few feet from the window. I ran ahead on my tiptoes and ducked behind the tree's broad trunk.

Quentin followed me. Then Haley. From there, we could see into the kitchen.

Then I think it sank in for all of us. Dirt's footprints ended right here! At the house of Off-Her-Rocker Crocker.

Tea for Two
2:10 P.M.

Behind the tree, we could see Mrs. Crocker moving about her kitchen. In one hand, she held a plastic bag full of something. In the other hand was a small, brown bottle.

The window above her sink was open. So when Mrs. Crocker turned on the water, we could see her wrinkled face. Long, gray hair spread out over thin, bony shoulders.

"She's mixing something," Quentin said.

The woman shook the bottle. Then she placed the bag in the sink. I held my breath as she pulled out a big, wooden mallet. *Wham!* She pounded the bag over and over.

"She's mixing an evil potion!" Haley said.

Quentin turned and glared at her. "Shhh!"

"Look," I said. "She's talking to some-body."

We couldn't make out all the words. But through the open window came, "Drink every drop, or else!" She turned and shook her finger toward the kitchen corner.

I thought I was imagining everything. It was just like Hansel and Gretel. And this was the gingerbread house! That meant Dirt would be in the oven!

My heart felt like it was trying to climb through my throat. "She's got Dirt!" I said. I started for the house.

Quentin put his arm out to stop me. "Wait! She's talking to Dirt again." All we could see was Mrs. Crocker. But we knew she had to be talking to poor Dirt.

"Drink, small one," she said. "Or I will make you …"

I couldn't stand it anymore. I jumped to my feet and ran to the door. My fists pound-ed it.

"Open up!" I screamed. "We know you've got Dirt! Let her go!"

I felt Quentin behind me. I didn't know if Haley was there or not. Then I heard *click, click, click.* And the door slowly cracked open.

A long, pointed nose poked through the crack. "What do you want?" asked Mrs. Crocker. Her voice was high. It snapped at me like a whip.

"We want Dirt!" I said.

"Eh?" She stuck her face into the crack.

"You know who we mean. Dirt!" My heart was pounding hard.

Something passed over the old woman's face. It was a smile. A warm, real smile. For a minute I didn't know what to do. Here I was. Ready to storm the house and rescue my friend. I wasn't ready for a smile.

Quentin was elbowing me. "Molly," he whispered, "look."

I looked through the open door where Quentin was pointing. Two raccoons were lapping up something from a bowl.

"She was talking to the coons!" Quentin whispered.

I gazed up at Mrs. Crocker. She was still smiling. "May I help you?" she asked.

"I—er—I mean—" I cleared my throat.

"Are you looking for Dirt?" she asked.

All I could do was nod.

"I was wondering where Dirt was myself.

Come inside."

I'm not supposed to go inside strangers' houses. I didn't move.

Mrs. Crocker seemed to understand. "How about if I come out?" she said. She stepped onto the porch. Haley was at the bottom of the steps. She backed away.

"I'm Molly Mack," I said. "This is Quentin."

"I'm Anna Crocker, better known as Off-Her-Rocker Crocker." She smiled again. I felt awful for ever calling her that.

It smelled like rain. But the birds were still chirping. They stop before a big storm. So I figured we still had time. "Have you seen Dirt?" I asked.

Mrs. Crocker looked at her watch. "No. And she should have been here by now. Last night when she left Winnie and Rick with me—"

"Winnie and Rick?" Quentin asked.

"Yes. The raccoons. Dirt said she'd be by for tea as usual."

"Wait a minute," I said. "You lost me."

Mrs. Crocker pulled her shawl tighter around her shoulders. "Dirt brought the raccoons by late last night. She said a dog got their mother. The babies were doing poorly.

Dirt asked me to see what I could do. I was just mixing some of my special herbs from my garden."

So that's the potion, I thought. "And she hasn't been by today?"

"No."

"Oh yeah?" Haley said. "Then why did Dirt's footprints lead us here?" She still stood a few feet away from us.

"Mrs. Crocker," I said, "this is Haley, Dirt's sister."

Mrs. Crocker raised her eyebrows. "Why, Dirt never said she had a sister. Imagine that!"

I tried to explain to Haley what I'd figured out about Dirt's footprints. "Dirt must have left those tracks last night, Haley."

I turned back to Mrs. Crocker. "How long have you known Dirt?" I asked.

"My," she said, "I suppose she's been coming here for tea for over a year now."

"Did she say *tea?*" Haley asked.

"Why, yes. Dirt helps in my herb garden. She's becoming quite an expert in herbs and tea."

We thanked Mrs. Crocker and said good-bye. I was glad we'd been wrong about her. But we still weren't any closer to finding Dirt.

This time I took the long way back with Quentin and Haley.

"You know," said Haley, "maybe we've got it wrong. Maybe Dirt ran away from home."

"But why would she?" I asked.

Haley thought a minute. Then she said, "Tonsils! Dirt's supposed to get her tonsils out. Maybe she ran away because she was scared."

"Not Dirt," I said. "Nothing scares her."

"More likely, it would be the doctor who ran away from home," Quentin said. "He would be taking a great risk to stick his hands down Dirt's throat."

We crossed the woods to Cinnamon Drive, Haley and Dirt's street. We were almost jogging. "Haley, when will your mother get home?" I asked.

"No fair!" Haley said. "You can't tell Mother. We have to find Dirt ourselves. Besides, Mother's at work."

"At least tell your baby-sitter, Haley," I said. "Don't you think—"

"Hey, look!" Quentin was pointing to something by the Harrisons' house. "It's an envelope."

A long, white envelope was taped to the front door. We ran to see it.

On the front of the envelope, printed in weird letters, was:

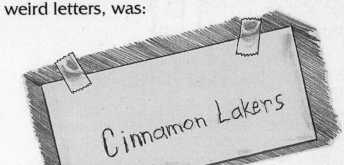

Cinnamon Lakers

I grabbed the envelope and tore it open. Instead of a letter, out poured an envelope full of *dirt!*

No Joke

2:30 P.M.

Quentin and Haley and I stared at the little mound of black dirt.

"What is it?" Haley asked.

"Dirt," Quentin said.

"What's it mean, Quentin?" I asked.

Quentin squatted down on the sidewalk and took a pinch of dirt from the pile. He sniffed it. Then he rubbed his fingers together. "Hmmm."

"Do you think it's from Dirt?" I asked. "Do you think she's playing a joke on us?"

"If she is," Haley said, "will she be sorry!"

I still held the white envelope. I turned it over to look for clues. "Hey!" I shouted. "Look! Something is on the back of the

envelope."

Quentin and Haley crowded around me. On the back flap of the envelope were three drawings. A circle that wasn't quite a circle. A tree. And a house. The house had a big *X* drawn over it.

"I'll bet it *is* from Dirt!" Haley whined. "She doesn't know how to write, so she drew pictures."

It was as if somebody kicked me in the stomach. I thought about Dirt asking me to help her write *S*'s. It hurt to remember how I turned her down.

What was Dirt trying to tell us? "I don't get it," I said. I studied the pictures. "Circle-tree-no house."

"It doesn't look like a circle to me," said Haley.

"Haley's right," Quentin said. "Even Dirt

could make it rounder. Unless ... perhaps what we have here is a body of water. A pond? A lake?"

A lake. A tree. No house. "Of course!" I screamed. "That's it! Cinnamon Lake tree house! *Our* tree house. All tree—no house! Get it?"

I knew I was right. We call our Cinnamon Laker clubhouse a tree house. But since we can't get our parents to help us build anything, so far it's all tree.

I stuffed the envelope into my pocket and took off for our Cinnamon Lake tree. I could not wait to see Dirt. I'd apologize. I'd help her do her *S*'s. And maybe I'd still have time to make the tryouts.

"Molly!" Quentin called after me.

I yelled over my shoulder at the slow-pokes. "I can't wait. See you there!" I didn't stop running until I reached the tree house. "Dirt!" I called, panting. "Dirt! Where are you?"

I slid down the little hill to our tree. Still no sign of Dirt.

"Come on, Dirt! You can come out now. I'm sorry I didn't help you. Let's practice *S*'s."

All I heard were crickets and the first rumble of thunder in the distance. It was getting colder by the minute. I stood at the base of our tree. "Dirt! I'm not kidding! This isn't funny anymore."

Staring up through the branches, I spied something white on the highest branch. *My* branch for all Cinnamon Laker meetings. As fast as I could, I climbed straight up. At the very top, somebody had placed another white envelope!

Again I ripped open the envelope. No dirt this time. I pulled out a folded sheet of paper. Letters had been cut from magazines and pasted to the page. I read it:

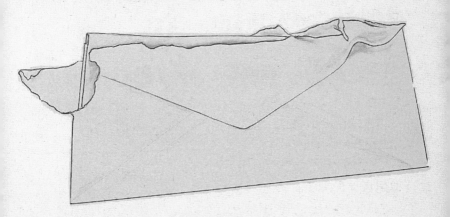

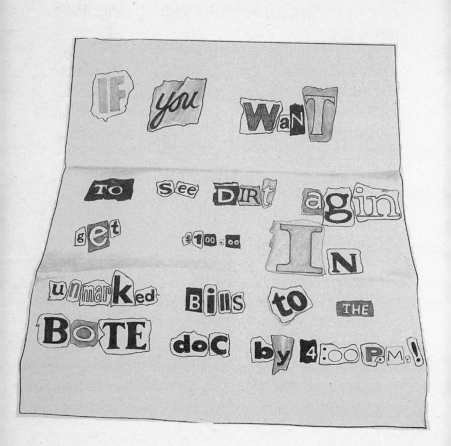

I was still in shock when Haley and Quentin arrived.

"Dirt! Molly?" Quentin yelled.

"Now Molly's gone too," Haley whined. "If *she's* missing, there's no way it's my fault."

"I'm up here," I called.

"And where, may I ask, is Dirt?" Quentin asked.

"Dirt's been kidnapped!"

"Kidnapped?!" Quentin yelled.

Haley started to cry.

I climbed down and let them read the ransom note.

"Quentin," I said, "where can we get $100? And by 4:00!"

"Hmmm. Allow me to see exactly what we have here." Quentin slid his glasses up on his nose. Then he took the note from me. "What we have here is a case of bad spelling. *A-g-i-n? B-o-t-e? D-o-c?*"

My little gray cells were trying to tell me something. Something was fishy here. How did the kidnappers know where our clubhouse is? How did they know we call it a tree house, even though there's no house?

"Quentin," I said, "are you thinking what

I'm thinking?"

"What?" Haley asked. "What are you thinking that Quentin's thinking?"

Quentin and I frowned at each other. "Vultures!" we said.

I should have guessed it before! Sam and Ben Benson and Quentin's cousin Marty have a real clubhouse on the other side of the lake. Those Vultures will do anything to make our lives miserable.

"You mean the Vultures kidnapped Dirt?" Haley asked.

"It sure looks that way," I said.

"So how do we get her back before Mother knows she's missing?" Haley whined.

"I do not trust my irresponsible cousin Martin to use good sense," said Quentin. "Martin rules his life by greed. If he does not get the money by four o'clock, I do not know what might happen to Dirt."

"But we don't have the money!" Haley said. "What are we going to do?"

My gray cells were working hard now. We *had* to rescue Dirt from the Vultures. "We'll take them the money," I said.

"Huh?" said Haley.

Quentin didn't get it either. "Molly, if we

leave something besides money at the boat dock, the Vultures will know."

"But they won't know right away," I said. "We can use the little case I got from Granny. It has a lock. And I'll keep the key."

"Hmmm," Quentin said, scratching his head. "Yes. I suspect the Vultures lack honor. They will not leave Dirt at the dock whether we leave the money or not. If they cannot open the case, they may lead us to Dirt."

"Exactly," I said.

"But then what?" Haley asked. "You can't expect us to take on the Vultures! Marty? Ben? Sam? Maybe even Eric the Red!"

But this time, I was ahead of them. "I think I have a plan," I said.

"You think?" Quentin asked.

"We've got to work fast!" My mind was racing in a million directions. "Haley, get your Monopoly money. Quentin, we'll need your telescope. Meet in 10 minutes at the docks. And hurry!"

Kid Napping
2:55 P.M.

Quentin and I hid behind a rowboat by the docks.

"Where on earth is Haley?" I whispered. "If she doesn't get here soon—"

"There she is!" Quentin said.

Haley stumbled across the pebbles down to the docks. She was carrying a large, white box.

I waved to her. "This way!"

Haley started down, slipped, and fell at our feet. The box lid blew off. Monopoly money flew everywhere.

"You didn't have to bring the whole game, Haley!" I chased fake $10s, $20s, $50s, $100s, and $500s.

We got most of it back. I opened my suit-case. We stuffed in the Monopoly money. The case was really a doll trunk. But I didn't want anybody to know I still played with dolls.

"Molly," Quentin said, "I fear not even the Benson bullies will believe this is real money."

"Yeah," I said, slamming the doll case shut. "But they won't know until it's too late."

I locked the trunk. "Who's going to make the drop?"

"Huh?" Haley said.

"The money drop. That's what kidnappers call it," I said, feeling like I had to explain everything to them. "Which one of us should leave the money on the dock?"

Somehow I was elected. Holding tight to the trunk, I made my way to the boat dock. Nobody was there. Not even a bird. In fact, the birds had stopped singing. Probably gone into hiding before the storm broke.

I set the trunk down gently and backed away. Then I ran back to Quentin and Haley. "Quentin," I said, "did you bring your tele-scope?"

Quentin pulled the telescope from his

jacket and handed it to me. "Molly, you must be careful. This is an important instrument for my work."

It worked great! When I looked through the telescope, I could see right inside the window of the Vultures' clubhouse.

"Wow," I said. "What a clubhouse!"

"Let me see!" Haley said. She grabbed the telescope. "No fair! We get hard branches. They get couches."

Quentin took the telescope from Haley. "I see a poster of giant vultures circling. And evidence of untidy behavior. Why, they have a refrigerator in there! Probably filled with cookies and ice cream. There's a TV. And a microwave. And—"

"But do you see Dirt?" I asked. Then I noticed the boat dock. The trunk was gone! "Quentin, they picked it up!"

Quentin swung the telescope around and scanned the dock. "Yes, I see him."

"Who?" I said. "Who is it?"

"It's difficult to tell. Someone in a raincoat and hat."

"No fair! Now what will we do?" Haley whined. "They have the money. And we still don't have Dirt."

"I didn't think they'd play fair," I said. "So I brought something along to even the sides."

"Nuclear weapons?" Quentin asked.

"Not quite," I said. I pulled out my secret key chain. "Chuckie got it for me last Christmas. It's an alarm chain! See? You press this green button for a buzzer sound. Press the white button, and it sounds like machine guns. But the red button is our secret weapon."

I put my thumb on the red button. "Okay. Ready to charge the Vulture clubhouse and rescue Dirt?"

Quentin and Haley didn't act ready. I wished I had Dirt to help rescue Dirt. She would have led the charge.

"Okay," I said. I took a deep breath. "Let's pray first. Dear God, we need your help. We're not big enough to scare the Vultures off. Please help us. Amen."

"Ready. Set. Raid!" And I hit the button.

Loud machine gun fire rang out.

"Oops," I said. "Wrong button."

I pressed the red button. This time, sirens rang out all around us. It sounded like a dozen police cars were surrounding the place.

The door of the Vultures' clubhouse burst open. Ben was the first one out. Then Marty, using Ben as a shield. Eric the Red ran out and banged into Marty, who bumped into Ben. Ben fell face first into a bush. Marty and Eric took off into the woods. Ben stumbled up and chased after them.

"It worked!" I cried. "We did it!"

The three of us raced to the clubhouse to get Dirt. I got there first. I peered inside. What I saw made me stop and blink. I couldn't be seeing right.

Somebody was tied to a cot. But it wasn't Dirt. It was Sam Benson! Around his neck was a cardboard sign. It said:

Beware Kid Napping!

Thinking Backwards
3:01 P.M.

"Sam Benson!" I screamed. "What are you doing here?"

Quentin and Haley stood at the door, as if they thought Vultures might still be inside.

"Where's Dirt?" Haley asked.

"Why is Samuel lying down?" Quentin came in behind me.

Sam pulled at the ropes. But his hands and feet were tied to the cot. "Would somebody please untie me? And get this stupid sign off?"

Quentin crossed the floor and lifted off Sam's sign. *"Kid Napping,"* he read. "An attempt at humor?"

I started untying the ropes. "You better tell

us where Dirt is, Sam Benson."

"I don't know where she is, Molly. Honest!"

"I'll bet," Haley mumbled. She still hadn't set foot in the clubhouse.

"No fooling," Sam said. "We haven't seen Dirt. We figured she'd turn up. Marty just thought he might make a few bucks before she did."

"So you were in on the *kid napping,*" I said. I untied the last rope and threw it at him.

"Nah," he said. "Well, not really. I mean, I found out about it. But look what they did to me. They were afraid I'd mess it up." Sam sat on the edge of the cot. "I didn't think you'd really worry about Dirt. That kid is one tough cookie."

"Well, I *am* worried," I said. "Now we're back to no leads. All we've found out is that Ben and Marty didn't take her. She rescues raccoons. She takes care of bats. And she drinks tea with Mrs. Crocker."

"Off-Her-Rocker Crocker?" Sam asked.

"But nobody's seen Dirt." I didn't feel like explaining to Sam.

"You're really worried, aren't you?" Sam

said. He stared at me. "Come on. Where should we look next?"

"We?" I said. I still didn't know if I should trust Sam Benson. He could be pretty nice when he wanted to. I'd even told him about Jesus once. But I also had seen him make fun of people behind their backs.

"Look," Sam said, as if he knew what I was thinking. "The Vultures haven't exactly done me any favors lately. Besides, the more people looking for Dirt, the better. Right?"

"Not if the people are Vultures," Quentin said. But he sat down with Sam and me.

I tried to remember the detective stories I'd read. "Sometimes," I said slowly, thinking, "detectives have to start thinking backwards."

"Backwards?" Quentin said. "The gray cells do not work backwards."

"I mean, like when was the last time anybody saw Dirt? Haley, which way was Dirt walking when she got off the bus?"

"Umm, she ... er ... I don't know," Haley said.

"We realize you do not have a firm grasp on geography, Haley," Quentin said. "We do not need to know if she went north, south, east, or west. Simply tell us if she was walking toward your house or away from it."

"It's not that, smart aleck," Haley said. "I can't remember seeing Dirt after I got off the bus."

"*I* did not see her," Quentin said. "I was reading."

"I was getting killed by jelly beans," Sam said.

"Well, I didn't see her either," I said. "I was working on my play lines."

It was the first time since the kidnap note that I'd thought about tryouts. Dorothy and Oz didn't seem important anymore. "Didn't anybody see Dirt get off the bus?" I asked.

Haley and Sam and Quentin shook their heads.

"Think backwards!" I said. "On the bus, who saw her last?"

The last time I'd seen Dirt, I'd yelled at her. I had to find her now and tell her how sorry I was.

"I know!" Sam said. "I saw her when the jelly beans spilled. She got a big handful!"

"All right, then," I said. "Now we're getting somewhere."

"I'll bet Dirt got off the bus early!" Haley said. "She's always getting off at other kids' stops. She says she likes walking home. It would be just like her to get off early and let me get in trouble for it."

Finally I felt we were on our way to finding Dirt. "Let's split up," I said. "We can start with the last bus stop before Cinnamon Lake. The Sloan farm."

"I'll take the Sloan farm," Haley called. Not only was that the closest place, but Michael Sloan lived there. Michael's in sixth grade. Haley almost falls over herself whenever he walks by.

"Quentin, you've got the Jacobs' house." I gave him the next closest house because he's not the fastest person I know. I could see him breathe a sigh of relief.

Sam took Harts' and I settled for McCarthys'.

"Let's meet on route 620 after we check our stops," I said. "And let's all pray we find Dirt safe and sound."

It was a quiet take-off for third graders. I guess we all had our own thoughts about Dirt. I was thinking that I'd known all along Dirt really *was* my responsibility. No matter what I'd said on the bus.

In Sunday school we'd just learned, "Let

us love one another, for loves comes from God." And God loved us so much He sent His Son Jesus to die for us. I felt almost that much love for Dirt right now. All I wanted was a chance to tell her.

Bus Stop, Bus Stop,
Who's Got the Bus Stop?
4:09 P.M.

We left the clubhouse in search of missing Dirt. Since Harts and McCarthys live on the same road, Sam and I ended up walking together. More like running together.

"It's getting so cold, Molly," Sam said. "Do you suppose Dirt had … *has* … a jacket?"

"You know Dirt," I said. "She probably doesn't even have shoes. We just have to find her, Sam."

"She'll be okay, Molly," Sam said.

We were going straight into the wind. I had to lean forward to keep moving. At the top of a long hill, Sam and I split up.

"There's Harts'," Sam said. He headed for

the farm on the right.

Erin McCarthy's house was across the road. I ran all the way there. A big, black sheep dog came out and barked at me.

I knocked. "Mrs. McCarthy! Erin!"

I rang the doorbell. A little song played. But nobody came. I left the porch and walked around the house to the garage. "Yoo hoo! Anybody home?"

But nobody was home. Disappointed, I went back and waited for Sam. Each second made me more and more scared for Dirt. A big roll of thunder shook the earth. Then I saw Sam running toward me.

"Sam!" I hollered. "Have they seen her?"

Sam didn't seem to hear me over the thunder. When he got closer, he said, "No luck?"

I shook my head. "Were Harts home?" I asked.

"Yeah. But they never saw her."

We started walking back to 620. I couldn't think of anything to say. Anything to do.

"Maybe Quentin and Haley have Dirt right now," Sam said. "She probably has some funny story about where she's been."

I knew he was trying to cheer me up. But I

couldn't help it. It was as if Dirt had disappeared.

"Wait a minute!" Sam said. "What about Mr. Winkle? Maybe he saw Dirt get off the bus."

"That's a great idea, Sam! Let's go ask him."

Sam and I had to cross two cornfields and a mess of barbed wire to reach Mr. Winkle's place. Sam ran right up to the door and started knocking. I joined him and banged the door with both fists.

"Mr. Winkle! Mr. Winkle!" I yelled.

I heard a chain rattle. Then a click, click, click. Slowly, the door cracked open. The eye and nose of Mr. Winkle appeared in the crack.

"Open up, Mr. Winkle," I said. "It's me, Molly Mack. It's real important!"

We stayed like that another minute. Then the door opened halfway. Mr. Winkle stood there in a white T-shirt and green slacks. He tugged his belt up to his waist. It made me think of trying to scoot a rubber band to the middle of a grapefruit.

"What is it?" he asked as if we were aliens from another planet.

"What's the fuss, Willie?" asked a tall, thin

woman. She must have been his wife. She was as skinny as Mr. Winkle was fat.

"*Mrs.* Winkle?" I asked, surprised. Mr. Winkle had a Mrs. Winkle? The jingle rang through my mind: "Jack Sprat could eat no fat. His wife could eat no lean." Only the Winkles had the roles mixed up.

"What do you want with my wife?" Mr. Winkle asked. He stuck out his arm to bar Mrs. Winkle from the doorway.

"No, no," I said. "We don't want Mrs. Winkle."

Mrs. Winkle looked hurt.

"I mean, we'd probably love Mrs. Winkle. She seems like a very nice—I mean ..."

Sam took over. "What we want, Mr. and Mrs. Winkle, is Dirt."

"Dirt?" repeated Mrs. Winkle. "And you thought the place to come for dirt was my house?" Mrs. Winkle pushed her way into the doorway and past Mr. Winkle. "What has Willie been telling you?" she asked.

Mrs. Winkle turned on her husband. "A little dust on top of the television. And all of a sudden I'm a horrible housekeeper? Why, Willie Winkle, I—"

"Not dirt dirt," I yelled. "Dirt!"

Mrs. Winkle looked baffled.

"Mr. Winkle," I pleaded, "you've got to help us. Dirt Harrison, Haley's little sister, is missing. Have you seen her? Did you see her get off the bus?"

Mr. Winkle opened the door wide. "Dirt? Didn't she get off with you at Cinnamon?"

"No," I said. "And we can't find her anywhere."

"Oh, dear," Mrs. Winkle said. "A child is missing? A child called Dirt? Why would anyone name a child Dirt? No wonder the poor dear ran away!"

"Then you don't have any idea where she is?" Sam asked.

But I could see Mr. Winkle didn't know anything. "No," he said. "But if we see her, we'll bring her right home. Is there anything else we can do?"

"Pray," I said.

Then Sam and I left. Neither of us spoke. But I knew we were both hoping Quentin and Haley had found Dirt. And both of us knew in our hearts, they hadn't.

The Lost Is Found
4:25 P.M.

It wasn't until Sam and I had crossed the Winkles' pastures that I realized how dark it had gotten. Thunder came in rolls that grew closer and closer together.

When we hit 620, we saw Quentin and Haley. Haley was hugging herself and dancing to keep warm. We didn't have to ask. They hadn't found Dirt.

"Nobody's seen Dirt," Haley whined.

"Not a trace?" Sam asked.

"Well, we did gather a bit of information," Quentin said. "Mrs. Jacob says Dirt comes out there every other night. Something has been killing their chickens. Dirt watches to see if she can scare the beast off."

The girl was even more amazing than I thought.

"Michael Sloan said Dirt comes there before dawn every morning," Haley reported. "She feeds their lambs from a bottle! And she gives pizza to Michael's dog!"

We were quiet a minute. In awe of Dirt.

"Man," Sam said. "When does that girl sleep?"

And that's when my gray cells kicked in. "That's it!" I screamed.

I turned on my heels and took off running as fast as I could.

"Molly?" Quentin hollered after me.

"Winkles!" I shouted.

A huge drop of water splatted on my nose. At first I thought someone threw it at me. But it fell from the dark sky. Then another drop. And another. And soon it was pouring!

I ran through the rain. Across pastures, under barbed wire.

"Wait up!" I heard Sam shout.

They were running behind me. But I couldn't wait. The rain came so hard I had to squint. It was like swimming underwater with my eyes open. I saw Winkles' house ahead of me. My shoe slid in the mud. I felt my feet slide out from under me. Down I fell. Covered with mud, I picked myself up.

"Molly!" Sam called through the rain. He had caught up with me. "You okay? Why Winkles? They said they haven't seen Dirt."

"Come on," I told him. I banged on Winkles' door. This time it opened right away.

"Mr. Winkle!" I said. "Could we check the bus?"

Haley and Quentin came up the porch steps. We were all soaked. Quentin was panting. Haley was sneezing.

"You think the little girl is on my bus?" Mr. Winkle asked, his eyes wide, his mouth open.

"When does the girl sleep?" Quentin repeated Sam's question out loud. He had put the clues together too. "Of course!" Quentin cried. "Mr. Winkle! We must see that bus this instant."

But Mr. Winkle was already out the door. He didn't even bother with an umbrella or a raincoat. He led us at a trot. We splashed through the mud to the barn.

"This is where I keep my bus," Mr. Winkle explained.

We waited for him to shove the barn door

open. Mrs. Winkle joined us, her coat over her shoulders like a cape. Her pink hair curlers dripped with rain.

The barn door slid open. There was our big, gold school bus, surrounded by hay. The bus windows were fogged, so I couldn't see inside.

"With the motor off, there's no way to open her from the inside." Mr. Winkle pushed the middle of the door. It folded open.

Sam and I nearly knocked over Mr. Winkle as we pushed past him.

It was so dark inside the bus, it took a minute for my eyes to get used to it. I could feel jelly beans under my feet.

"Hey! 'Bout time," barked a little, scruffy voice.

I looked toward the voice. It was Dirt!

"Dirt!" I screamed. She was sitting in the back seat, munching on jelly beans. I ran up to her and hugged her.

I breathed deeply and thanked God for leading us to Dirt and keeping her safe.

Then everybody—Quentin, Haley, Mr. and Mrs. Winkle—crowded around Dirt.

"Dirt!" Haley cried. "We were so worried! We looked everywhere! What are you doing

in here?"

"Sleeping," Dirt said, frowning up at us. "And eating." She popped another jelly bean into her mouth.

Dirt shook off our hugs. "But thanks for coming." She got to her feet. "Well, gotta go. It's getting dark." Dirt started down the aisle. I had to run to catch up with her.

"Dirt," I said, "I'm sorry I was mean. I'll help you with your *S*'s. Let's go do it now."

Dirt hopped off the bus. I kept up with her. "Cool," she said.

Mr. and Mrs. Winkle stayed shivering inside the bus. Haley, Quentin, and Sam jumped down behind me.

"You made me miss the tryouts, Dirt!" Haley said. "Now Mr. Adams will give Dorothy's part to Ashley. No fair!"

I had forgotten all about the Wizard of Oz. With Dirt standing there, safe, I figured I could get by another year without being a star.

We crossed the barn. The rain fell in sheets. Big drops blew into the barn through the open door. Dirt didn't even slow down.

"Dirt and I are going back and work on *S*'s," I announced.

"Later," Dirt said. "First, I got responsibilities. I'm late for tea."

And with that, Dirt took off into the pouring rain.

I stood staring after her. Then she turned and looked over her shoulder. For just a minute, our eyes held each other. Without a word, it was like Dirt was saying, "Thanks, Molly. I knew you'd come through for me."

And without a word, I was saying, "It's okay, Dirt. I know. You *are* my responsibility."

Then Dirt whipped her head around. She raced off, splashing through puddles and out of sight.

"Where's she going?" Sam asked.

"How should I know?" Haley whined. "Am I my sister's keeper?"

Quentin, Sam, and I looked at each other. "Yes!" we cried.

Solve more mysteries
with the Cinnamon Lakers!

Enjoy reading
The Secret Society of the Left Hand,
available at your local Christian bookstore.